The Treasure of Mr Tipp

The Treasure of Mr Tipp

Margaret Ryan

Illustrated by Kate Pankhurst

A & C Black • London

For Angus with love

First published 2009 by
A & C Black Publishers Ltd
36 Soho Square, London, W1D 3QY

www.acblack.com

Text copyright © 2009 Margaret Ryan
Illustrations copyright © 2009 Kate Pankhurst

The rights of Margaret Ryan and Kate Pankhurst to be identified as
the author and illustrator of this work have been asserted by them in
accordance with the Copyrights, Designs and Patents Act 1988.

ISBN 978-1-4081-0494-1

A CIP catalogue for this book is available from the British Library.

The problem: My old bike. I am growing too big for it, but we can't afford a new one as Dad is off work with a broken leg.

The brainwave: Ask Mr Maini at the corner shop if he has a paper round so I can save up for some new wheels.

The dilemma: There is a paper round, but it takes in Weir Street and I've heard that the people who live there are weird.

The hero: Me, of course. Jonny Smith. I'm not scared – it's only a paper round. And just how weird can the people in Weir Street be…?

Chapter One

I'm an ordinary sort of boy. I live in an ordinary house, with ordinary windows and doors. I have an ordinary dog, an ordinary cat and an ordinary goldfish. My family are ordinary, too, if you don't count my little sister, Ellie, who could win Olympic medals if eating was a sport.

I like ordinary things like football, computer games and school holidays. I'm not too keen on school, though, or my teacher, Miss Dodds. She thinks my head is full of nonsense. And she doesn't believe me when I tell her about the extraordinary things that happen in Weird Street.

I don't think she's ever been there. Or, if she has, she probably just whizzes up and down the hill in her car, thinking up difficult maths problems. I bet she doesn't notice the people or the houses. But when I'm on my paper round, I notice the people *and* the houses, especially when they're a little bit odd ... like number 34 and a half.

❧

"Don't you think that's a strange number for a house?" I asked Mr Maini one day, as he wrote it on the corner of the newspaper.

Mr Maini just shrugged. "Some people call their houses strange names, so why not strange numbers."

I didn't argue with him, but number 34 and a half is a very odd house. It stands halfway up Weird Street and looks like it's come from the pages of a storybook.

The whole thing has been dug right out of the hillside, probably by a huge bulldozer. It has an old oak door covered in iron studs, with a big, iron bell, and its windows are made from the bottoms of bottles. Strangest of all is its flat roof, where vegetables grow. Rows and rows of them.

The first time I saw the house I thought that a giant lived there. An untidy giant who kept broken fridges, and prams and washing machines in his garden.

As I dodged around the junk on my way to the front door, I half expected to find a large beanstalk spiralling up towards the clouds, or a brown hen clucking about, laying golden eggs.

No such luck. All I found was more junk. But I *didn't* find a letter box. There wasn't one on the door, so I yanked on the old bell instead.

I heard a clang, then a muffled explosion came from inside the house.

"What have I done?" I gasped.

I quickly stuck the paper into an empty old milk churn and scurried away.

❧

"Who lives at number 34 and a half?" I asked Mr Maini when I handed back my bag. "I rang the bell and there was an explosion. Did I do something wrong?"

Mr Maini smiled. "Oh no, that would just be Mr Tipp inventing something. He's always making new things out of the rubbish people throw away."

Ah! That explained the noise *and* the junk in the garden.

"Trouble is," said Mr Maini, "sometimes

Mr Tipp blows up bits of his house … and himself, too. He lost a door and half an eyebrow last week."

"I haven't seen him yet," I said.

"You will," smiled Mr Maini, and would say no more.

Of course that made me really curious. I couldn't wait to find out more about Mr Tipp and I couldn't wait to meet him.

❧

Then one morning I got my chance.

As I approached number 34 and a half, I saw that the old oak door was lying open. I know I should have just delivered the paper and left, but I didn't. I tiptoed inside and found myself in a large, dimly lit hall.

I peered through the gloom. YIKES! I was not alone! The hall was full of robots standing stiffly to attention. They were made entirely out of junk. Some of them had square faces, some had round, and the

12

light coming from the bottle-bottom
windows gave them an eerie, greenish glow.
I looked at them, my eyes wide. And, what
was really scary, they all seemed to look
rightback at me.

I gasped and was about to go when one
of the robots, wearing tinfoil overalls and
an old diver's helmet, suddenly moved.

"Do come in," it said in a hollow voice.
"You're just what I need."

Chapter Two

I stood stock still in the dim light, heart thumping, knees wobbling. "The… The… The door was open…" I managed to say.

The robot reached up and took off its diver's helmet. A kind face under some straggly white hair appeared. "Mr Tipp?" I asked faintly.

The man nodded. "Charlie can't have turned the handle properly when he closed the door," he said. "There's still a slight problem with his programming." I must have looked puzzled because Mr Tipp went on. "That's Charlie over there. The robot wearing the red rubber glove on his right hand. I thought it would improve his grip."

"Perhaps he's left-handed," I gulped.

"I hadn't thought of that," smiled Mr Tipp, stepping out of the tinfoil overalls to reveal a patchwork jersey and tartan trousers. "Tinfoil really does keep you warm, you know. This kind of suit might be useful for old people in the winter. Not sure about the diver's helmet, though. Better find another use for that."

"What about a goldfish bowl," I suggested. "I've heard that goldfish like a place to hide because they don't like being stared at all the time."

"Good idea," said Mr Tipp. "Now, who are *you*? No, don't tell me. You must be the paperboy. I've seen you puffing up the hill on your bike."

"I'm Jonny Smith," I said. "It's hard work riding my old bike – it's too small. So I'm saving up for a new one."

"I ride a three-wheeler that used to belong to my grandfather," smiled Mr Tipp. "We never throw anything away in our family."

I could believe that. There was stuff everywhere. "Do you make different kinds of robots?" I asked, gazing around.

Mr Tipp nodded. "Look over here. I've just finished making a scarobot to stop the birds eating the seeds on my roof garden."

I'd seen scarecrows in the fields before, but never anything like this. It looked like it was made from an old shop-window dummy. It was dressed in a plastic patchwork suit and a red bobble hat. On its feet were giant-sized wellies.

"The gent's outfitters in town was closing down," explained Mr Tipp. "They put this dummy out in their skip and I rescued it. Now, once the scarobot's on the roof, I'm going to fill these wellies with wet sand to weigh it down. But I'm not as young as I used to be and I need a hand to carry it up there. Right – you grab the head."

I did as I was told and we staggered out of the house. I held the scarobot while Mr Tipp fetched a ladder. Holding the dummy between us, we climbed onto the flat roof and placed it in the middle of the garden.

"Excellent," beamed Mr Tipp. "Now I'll pour the sand into the wellies while you go and fill the watering can. It's in the shed somewhere."

I climbed back down the ladder and looked for the shed. I found it hidden behind some overgrown brambles. It wasn't a proper shed, more like an old canvas igloo, and it was full of junk, too. Eventually, I found the watering can tucked inside an old tumble dryer. I filled it with water from the garden tap, then climbed back onto the roof.

"Well done," said Mr Tipp. "I've loaded the wellies with sand. You add the water while I make sure the scarobot's arms work." He took a remote-control device from his trouser pocket, pressed a red button, and the scarobot's arms moved up and down.

"Wow," I said.

Mr Tipp looked pleased. "What shall we call him? I like to give my robots names."

I looked at the scarobot's bobble hat. "How about Bob?"

"Bob it is," cried Mr Tipp. "I once had a teacher called Bob."

"Oh no," I cried. "A teacher! Miss Dodds! I have to go. I'll be late for school again." Then I raced down the ladder and jumped on my bike, waving to Mr Tipp as I did so.

Mr Tipp and Bob waved back. "Come again, Jonny Smith, and I'll show you some more of my inventions!"

"I will!" I yelled. Then I pedalled like the wind, only stopping to hand in my bag to Mr Maini.

"You've been a long time today," he said. "What kept you?"

"Tell you tomorrow. No time now," I panted, and scooted off.

The school playground was deserted when I got there, apart from a black-and-white collie, who couldn't read the NO DOGS ALLOWED sign.

I hurried to my classroom and tried to sneak in without anyone noticing, but Miss Dodds can hear a mouse sneeze, and anyway, the door creaks.

"You're late again, Jonny Smith," she frowned. "What fantastic excuse do you have this time?"

The class looked up expectantly, and my friends, Sara and Surinder, rolled their eyes.

"I was up on a roof garden watering the sand inside a scarobot's wellies," I said.

Miss Dodds' eyes narrowed. "Complete nonsense, as usual. You'll stay inside at break and write out six reasons why lying is very, very bad," she ordered.

I sighed deeply. I'd had a feeling she wouldn't believe me.

Chapter Three

At break, I took a piece of paper and started to do my punishment exercise.

SIX REASONS WHY LYING IS VERY, VERY BAD.

I wrote down the heading then thought really hard. Number one was easy.

1. LYING GETS YOU INTO TROUBLE.

After that it got trickier.

2. LYING GETS YOU INTO TROUBLE WITH YOUR TEACHER, EVEN IF YOU'RE NOT. (LYING, THAT IS.)

3. LYING GETS YOU INTO TROUBLE WITH YOUR FRIENDS WHO THINK YOU'RE AN IDIOT, EVEN IF THEY REALISE LATER THAT YOU'RE TELLING THE TRUTH.

After that it got trickier still.

4. LYING IS VERY, VERY BAD BECAUSE TELLING THE TRUTH IS VERY, VERY GOOD, THOUGH MY DAD LIES WHEN MY MUM ASKS HIM IF HER BUM LOOKS BIG IN HER JEANS.

It does.

5. LYING IS VERY, VERY BAD, ESPECIALLY IF YOU GET FOUND OUT.

After that I got really stuck so...

6. I KNOW LYING IS VERY, VERY BAD, BUT THE TRUTH IS I CAN'T THINK OF ANOTHER REASON. SORRY.

I left the piece of paper on Miss Dodds' desk. I saw her reading it later and her face kind of twitched. I didn't know whether that was good or bad, but I worked really hard for the rest of the day anyway.

At least Sara and Surinder believed me. They hadn't when I'd first told them about Captain Cross-eyed, the huge pirate that lives at number 13, but that *was* a very strange story. And, once they'd met him, they realised I was telling the truth.

Now Sara and Surinder were really keen to see what a scarobot looked like. So, after school, we all went to Weird Street. We stood at the gate of number 34 and a half and waved to Bob on the flat roof.

"Wow, that's magic," said Sara, when Bob waved back.

I didn't tell her that I thought Bob was programmed to wave every so often.

"I like his patchwork suit," said Surinder. "I wonder if Mr Tipp made that, too."

"Mr Tipp sounds really cool. I'd like to meet him," said Sara.

"Then you can," said a voice behind us, and Mr Tipp stopped his big three-wheeler bike at the side of the road.

The three of us stared open-mouthed. The bike was painted every colour of the rainbow and a trailer full of old junk was attached to it.

"I've been seaching through skips and rescuing treasure," beamed Mr Tipp. "You can help me unload it, if you like."

"I love your scarobot, Mr Tipp," said Sara, staggering into the garden with a long plank of wood.

"Have you invented lots of things?" gasped Surinder, clutching a box full of half-empty paint tins.

"Quite a few," smiled Mr Tipp. "I'm a bit busy right now, but come back on Saturday and I'll show you some of my inventions."

"Great," we agreed, and said goodbye.

When I got home, Mum and Ellie were out, Noggin, our cat, was curled up on the sofa and Dad was hopping about on his crutches, trying to plug in a new toaster.

"What have you done with the old one?" I asked.

"It's in the bin," said Dad.

I went outside and rescued it. "I know someone who would like this," I said, and told Dad all about Mr Tipp.

"I've seen him around town," smiled Dad. "You can't miss him, on that bike."

"We're going to visit him on Saturday. I'll take the toaster with me."

"Fine," said Dad. "But right now, you need to take Brutus for his walk."

I got Brutus's lead. "Come on," I said. "I'll take you up Weird Street and show you what a scarobot looks like."

But I couldn't.

When I got there, Bob had disappeared. Mr Tipp's roof garden was empty.

"That's funny," I said. "Bob was working perfectly an hour ago. Mr Tipp wouldn't have taken him down for no reason. Something must have happened."

Something certainly had.

Chapter Four

"Health and safety. That's what's happened," said Mr Tipp gloomily, when Sara, Surinder and I went over on Saturday. "Shortly after you left the other day, a silver car pulled up and Mr Gripe from the council knocked on my door. 'That figure on your roof is dangerous', he said. 'It might fall and hurt someone. It must be removed'."

"Didn't you tell him about the wet sand in the wellies?" I asked.

Mr Tipp nodded. "I offered to replace it with concrete, but it was no use. Bob still had to come down. I'll have to find another use for him. Perhaps I'll put him at the gate to wave at passers-by... But I promised to show you some of my inventions, didn't I. Would you like to come inside?"

"Yes, please," we chorused.

The four of us headed for the house and stopped outside.

"I'll just ring for the butler," smiled Mr Tipp. "This door used to belong to a ruined castle before I rescued it. The door, that is. Couldn't get the castle into the trailer."

He yanked on the iron bell and this time there was a loud clank, followed by some slow, scraping metal noises. Then the door creaked open and Charlie stood there, wearing his red rubber glove.

"You were right, Jonny," grinned Mr Tipp. "Charlie *is* left-handed."

We went into the gloomy hall and Sara and Surinder's mouths fell open when they saw the robots.

"What do they all do?" asked Surinder. "Well," said Mr Tipp, "my old legs and arms are getting a bit creaky, so they help me lift and carry things mostly. Though some of them have special jobs. Charlie's in charge of opening and closing the front door, Ben sweeps the floor, and Alice, the one with the mop head, switches on the kettle for tea."

"What's that over there?" asked Sara. She pointed to an old oil drum with a metal arm sticking out of it. Attached to the metal arm was a bone.

"Ah," smiled Mr Tipp. "That's my cure for overweight dogs. "Watch." He flicked a switch on the drum and the metal arm started going round and round. "The idea is that the dog chases the bone," he grinned. "The bone will go round faster and faster till the dog's had enough exercise. Then it stops and he gets his reward. Simple."

"I wonder if it works with chubby little sisters," I joked.

"Now, come into my workshop," said Mr Tipp. "I'll show you my latest invention. I think you'll like it."

We followed Mr Tipp through a small door at the far end of the hall and found ourselves in a very different kind of room. This one was brightly lit, with mirrors covering most of the walls. There were hall mirrors, dressing-table mirrors, even old wing mirrors.

Mr Tipp smiled as we pulled faces in them. "It's amazing the treasure people

throw out," he said. "The mirrors help to reflect the light. Now, have a look at this."

He led us to a big table, which was covered with test tubes and scientific instruments. Some coloured liquids bubbled and burped away quietly. I wondered what they were, and wished I'd listened more carefully in our science lessons.

Mr Tipp uncovered a large white bowl. Inside was a spongy blue mixture smelling of peppermint.

"What is it?" I asked.

"Boomerang chewing gum," beamed Mr Tipp. "Taste it." And he pulled bits off and handed them to us. "It's made mainly from the juice of the Sapodilla tree which grows in tropical America. It's perfectly safe. "

We popped the gum into our mouths. It tasted delicious.

"Why do you call it Boomerang chewing gum?" I mumbled.

Mr Tipp beamed even more. "Take it out of your mouth and throw it on the floor."

"What?"

"Go on," he instructed.

I took out the chewing gum and dropped it at my feet. Immediately, it bounced back into my hand.

"What did I tell you!" Mr Tipp jumped up

and down in delight. "Boomerang chewing gum. Throw it away and it comes right back."

Sara and Surinder tried it out, too.

"When you've finished chewing, you can play with it," they giggled.

Just then some white smoke starting curling up from the purple liquid in one of the test tubes.

"What's that?" I asked.

"The answer to smelly socks, I hope," said Mr Tipp. "But it's not quite right yet. When I sprayed it inside my socks, the local cats followed me for miles."

We grinned and followed Mr Tipp into the kitchen for tea. It was quite a normal kitchen, if you didn't count the fact that when Mr Tipp pressed his remote control, Alice came in and switched on the kettle.

We sat round the table with big mugs of tea and lots of chocolate biscuits, and talked about Mr Tipp's amazing inventions. Then Mr Tipp had to get back to his cure for smelly socks, so he and Charlie waved us off from the big oak door.

"What a pity Bob's not allowed to wave from the roof any more," I said.

We collected our bikes and were just leaving when a large, silver car arrived and stopped outside the gate. A man with a briefcase got out and headed towards Mr Tipp.

I saw Mr Tipp frown.

"I bet that was Mr Gripe," I said to Sara and Surinder. "I wonder what he wants now. I hope it doesn't mean more trouble for Mr Tipp."

But it did.

Chapter Five

After our visit to Mr Tipp, we headed into town to spend our pocket money. At least Sara and Surinder did, I was still saving up for my new bike.

We met Mum and Ellie and Gran in the shopping mall. Ellie was eating an ice cream while Mum and Gran signed a petition.

"It's for more bins in the town centre," said Mum. "These ones are overflowing."

"And they smell," declared Gran. "The streets are a disgrace. They weren't like that when I was a girl."

Sara, Surinder and I giggled. It was hard to imagine my gran ever being a girl. Gran smiled, too, and gave us some money for ice cream. We raced each other to the café, and took ages to decide what flavour we wanted. Then we strolled around, licking our cones and checking out the latest trainers. Surinder was thinking about buying a pair with his birthday money and disappeared inside a shop. Sara was heading to the library, so I cycled home.

Dad was just settling down on the sofa to watch some sport, but he listened carefully when I told him the story of Bob and Mr Gripe.

"Bob could have been a danger," he said.

"But Bob's been taken down, so why would Mr Gripe go back to see Mr Tipp?"

Dad shrugged. His favourite football team had just appeared on the screen and he had other things to think about.

But I didn't. I thought about the mystery of Mr Gripe all weekend, and still couldn't come up with an answer.

I'll get up extra early on Monday morning, I decided, and go and call on Mr Tipp. That way I'll find out what's going on.

But when I arrived at number 34 and a half, Mr Tipp was already outside on his three-wheeler bike, with his trailer piled high.

"You've been out rescuing treasure early today," I said.

Mr Tipp shook his head sadly." Not *rescuing*, Jonny," he said. "Getting rid off. I've got to take all this stuff to the dump. Mr Gripe was here on Saturday and he said

I have to clear everything out of my front garden."

"But why?" I said. "It's your garden."

"Health and safety again," said Mr Tipp. "Someone might come to the house and trip over it. And he said there had been lots of complaints from the neighbours about the mess."

"Yours isn't the only messy garden," I said. "What about the shoulder-high grass next door?"

But Mr Tipp just sighed and pedalled away.

I popped his paper in the milk churn and carried on with my round. When I got to number 13, I bumped into Captain Cross-eyed.

"Good morning, Jonny," he said. "You look a bit glum. Is something wrong?"

"It's Mr Tipp," I said, and told him the story.

"That's odd." Captain Cross-eyed frowned. "I know Mr Tipp's garden is a bit messy, but no one around here would ever complain. It's far too useful. He's always got spare parts for washing machines or lawn mowers, and he's always fixing things for people, too. Mr Tipp's a very kind and clever man."

"I know," I said. "But now he thinks the neighbours are complaining about him and he's really upset."

Then I had one of my brilliant brainwaves. That happens sometimes. I think I must have genius genes. I remembered the petition from Saturday. Perhaps the neighbours would sign something to get Mr Gripe to leave Mr Tipp alone.

I asked Captain Cross-eyed what he thought.

"Splendid idea," he said. "You write out the petition and I'll sign it. Better still, I'll go round the neighbours with you and get them all to sign, too."

I grinned as I pedalled off. No one would dare to argue with an enormous pirate.

❧

I was in good time for school. That pleased Miss Dodds. I got all my maths problems correct, too. That pleased her even more.

I scored a goal at football practice. That pleased Mr McGregor, who'd been threatening to drop me from the team. And *I* was pleased that we had art that afternoon. I like art. I'm quite good at it, so I don't usually get into any trouble…

Miss Dodds had pinned up a picture of Monet's *Water Lilies* for us to copy, and I'd finished mine in record time. It was quite like Monet's, except I had painted some large frogs on the lily pads.

I was just waiting for them to dry, when I spotted a spare piece of paper.

That would do for the petition, I thought. I could write it out while Miss Dodds was busy helping Sara. Sara is hopeless at art. She can't even draw a straight line with a ruler.

So I wrote out a petition like the one I had seen Mum and Gran sign. It said:

I was very pleased with that "valuable member of the community" bit, as I'd heard my dad say it about Captain Cross-eyed. Then I started to illustrate the edges by drawing some of Mr Tipp's robots. I put in Charlie, Ben, Mop-head Alice and Bob.

"Jonny Smith, what are you doing?"

Oh no! I hadn't heard Miss Dodds approach.

"Er, it's a petition," I said. "Captain Cross-eyed, who lives at 13 Weird Street, is going to take it round the neighbours with me. Mr Tipp, who lives at 34 and a half, is being asked by the council to clear up his garden because the neighbours are complaining about the junk... But they're not. Mr Tipp's an inventor who makes robots.

That's Charlie with his red rubber glove, who opens the front door; Ben, who sweeps the floor, though I've never actually seen him do that; and Mop-head Alice, who switches on the kettle. I've seen her do that. And that's Bob, the scarobot I told you about last week..." *When you didn't believe me, either*, I could have added.

Miss Dodds gave me one of her looks. The one that can turn your belly to jelly.

"If you persist with this silly storytelling, Jonny Smith," she said. "I will have to speak to your parents about it at parents' night. Have a think about it. The choice is yours."

YIKES!

Chapter Six

I put the petition in my pocket and cycled over to 13 Weird Street after tea. Captain Cross-eyed signed it, then we set off down the road.

When we arrived at number 19, there was a lady dressed in a pink, spangly leotard, doing handstands in her garden.

"That's Ursula Bend. She used to be a circus acrobat," whispered Captain Cross-eyed, as she began to spin cartwheels.

"Must keep in shape," she said, landing neatly in front of us. "Now, what can I do for you?"

When we explained, she signed the petition right away.

"I would never complain about Mr Tipp," she declared. "He fixed my leaky drainpipe. Now it's as good as new." And we left her swinging round and round on a lower branch of a big oak tree.

"A lot of interesting people live in Weird Street," I said to Captain Cross-eyed, who just nodded and smiled.

When we got to number 23, I pressed the bell. *DING DONG! DING DONG!* it boomed out, just like Big Ben. It gave me such a fright, I nearly jumped out of my socks.

"I should have warned you about that," said Captain Cross-eyed. "Mr Woyka is a clockmaker and he's a bit deaf."

An elderly gentleman with side whiskers opened the door. "Who are you?" he peered at me. "If you're selling something, I don't want it."

"We're not selling anything, Mr Woyka. We just want you to sign a petition to help Mr Tipp," bellowed Captain Cross-eyed.

"A petition? I never sign anything without reading it. Come in. I must find my glasses."

We went inside. No wonder Mr Woyka could hardly hear anything, the whole house was full of clocks, tick-tocking, chiming or cuckooing. An elderly lady sat in a rocking chair by the fire, conducting an imaginary orchestra.

"Rose," bellowed Mr Woyka. "Have you seen my glasses?"

Mrs Woyka did not reply, so Mr Woyka took off her headphones and asked again.

"You had them on when you were looking at old Tom."

"Ah," said Mr Woyka, and went over to the biggest of the grandfather clocks. He opened the case and felt inside. "Here they are. Must have slipped off when I wasn't looking." He put on a pair of very thick glasses and read the petition. "Of course I'll sign this," he said. "Mr Tipp makes the spare parts to keep old Tom going." He patted the clock affectionately. Then he gave the petition to his wife to sign, too.

"Right," said Captain Cross-eyed, when we left. "Now let's go to number 36 and see if Dr Sphinx is around."

"Number 36," I gulped. "That's the house with the shoulder-high grass. I have to go there on my paper round. I'm sure wild animals live there."

Captain Cross-eyed just laughed.

I felt a *bit* braver opening the gate with a large pirate by my side. But not much. I could hear strange rustling sounds in the undergrowth.

"Here, Tiger," called Captain Cross-eyed. *Tiger?*

A large cat with a stripy tail slid out of the long grass and wound himself round the captain's leg.

"Dr Sphinx has a lot of cats, but Tiger's my favourite."

More and more cats appeared until the captain and I were surrounded. Then the undergrowth rustled again and a man emerged. He wore jodhpurs, a shirt with lots of pockets, and a strange kind of hat.

"Dr Sphinx," said Captain Cross-eyed. "This is my young friend, Jonny Smith, and we need your help."

"Always happy to help," said Dr Sphinx, and listened to our story.

"It will be a pleasure to sign the petition," he said. "When Inca lost one of her legs in a car accident, Mr Tipp made her a new one. Look…"

I looked, and noticed for the first time that one of the cats had an artificial leg with a little wheel on the end.

"Cool," I said.

"Inca thinks so," smiled Dr Sphinx. He signed his name with a squiggle then disappeared back the way he had come.

It was the same at every house – the neighbours were very happy to sign their names. Even Miss King, with the very neat garden at number 57, agreed. None of them had complained about Mr Tipp's messy garden.

"So Mr Gripe told Mr Tipp a lie," I said. "My teacher says lying's very, very bad."

"It is," agreed Captain Cross-eyed. "Unless there's a very good reason for it."

"What reason could there possibly be?" I asked.

I was about to find out.

Chapter Seven

The next morning, I took the petition round to Mr Tipp.

"It's bound to cheer him up," I said to Mum and Dad, as I grabbed an apple and jumped on my bike.

But it didn't.

"It was very nice of the neighbours to sign this, Jonny," he said sadly. "But it's too late. This has just arrived."

He handed me a letter.

"It says my house is a danger to health and safety," he explained. "The council want to pull it down and put me in an old people's home. They don't think I can look after myself properly any more."

"But that's crazy," I said. "Anyway, you've got Charlie and Ben and Alice to help you…"

"Try explaining that to the council."

"I will," I said. "Or at least my dad will. Just you wait and see."

Mr Tipp smiled, but I could see he wasn't convinced.

Dad wasn't convinced, either. "If he really does need looking after, Jonny," he said quietly. "I don't think this petition will work."

"Sometimes they do," said Gran, who had come over for tea. "The one we signed the other day did. I heard from my friend, Mrs Bone, that we're going to get more bins in the town centre. Pity that won't help the mess the chewing gum makes on the pavements, though. Costs the council a fortune to clean *that* up."

"Mrs Bone?" I said. "Haven't I met her?"

Gran nodded. "She often presents the prizes at your school summer fête. Her husband owns the sweet factory."

That's when it hit me.

"Gran," I yelled. "You're a genius. I must get my genius genes from you!"

Thanks to Gran, I had just had another of my brainwaves.

I explained it to my family at length.

"Hmm, it might just work," said Dad. "Mr Bone's always on the look-out for new ideas. Shall we give it a try?"

"Anything to help Mr Tipp," I nodded, and crossed my fingers, my toes and my eyes.

Dad phoned Mr Bone and told him all about the Boomerang chewing gum. Mr Bone was very interested, and said he would like to meet Mr Tipp. So Dad phoned Mr Tipp and a meeting was arranged at number 34 and a half the next afternoon.

"Can I come, too?" I asked.

"Of course," said Dad. "It's all *your* idea."

After school, I cycled over to Weird Street. Dad and Mr Bone were sitting outside number 34 and a half in Mr Bone's big car.

"We waited for you," smiled Dad. "Jonny, meet Mr Bone."

"Hello, Jonny," said Mr Bone, and held out a long, skinny hand. "Your dad's been telling me all about you. You're obviously a clever lad."

Tell that to Miss Dodds, I thought.

We walked up to the house and I yanked on the big iron bell. After a few moments we heard some slow, scraping metal noises.

"That's Charlie, the butler," I said.

Charlie opened the door and we went inside.

"Come in, come in," said Mr Tipp, who was in the hall taking off Bob's wellies. "He doesn't need these now. I have to take him apart."

"Don't do that!" I cried. "Not yet. Not till you hear what my dad's got to say."

"Well, it was all Jonny's idea," smiled Dad, as he introduced Mr Bone. "As I told you on the phone, we're here to talk about your Boomerang chewing gum."

"Come through to my workshop," said Mr Tipp, and led the way. He went to the big table, uncovered the white bowl, and handed out chunks of the Boomerang chewing gum.

Mr Bone sniffed several times and then popped the chunk in his mouth. He chewed on the gum for ages, then took it from his mouth and threw it away.

"Fantastic!" he cried, when it bounced right back into his hand.

"I would definitely be interested in buying the recipe for this, Mr Tipp. There's a real market for it, I'm sure. But you'd need to make the chewing gum to begin with. I don't have room in my factory right now."

"Sorry." Mr Tipp shook his head sadly. "But I'd need my workshop to do that and the council say I have to leave my house."

Mr Bone smiled. "My wife is on the council. I'll tell her you're engaged in important scientific work that could help keep the streets clean. I'll tell her you must not be disturbed."

"So I'd never need to see Mr Gripe again?" beamed Mr Tipp.

"No," smiled Mr Bone.

Mr Tipp was delighted to be left in peace to get on with his inventions.

I was delighted, too. Mr Tipp had given me a whole bowl of Boomerang chewing gum. "Sell it to your friends and put the money towards your new bike, Jonny," he said. "You deserve it."

"Thank you," I grinned.

I took the chewing gum into school the next day, and told everyone about it.

"But how do we know it really comes back to you?" asked Peter Ho.

"I'll prove it," I said. Then I took a piece from my mouth and threw it at the classroom door.

But at that moment, the door opened and Miss Dodds came in. The chewing gum bounced off her nose and right back into my hand.

Miss Dodds held her nose and glared at me. "I hope you have a good explanation for this, Jonny Smith," she said. "And I want the truth. Not one of your fantastic tales."

Oh, help! Here we go again...

Just how weird can the people in Weir Street be?
Join Jonny on *all* his adventures…